Chair and Other Tales

Copyright © 2019 by Nic Pickle

Cover Art by Elizabeth "Richie" Urbina

All rights reserved. This book or any portion thereof may not be reproduced or used in any manner whatsoever without the express written permission of the publisher except for the use of brief quotations in a book review or scholarly journal.

First Edition

ISBN: 978-0-359-65515-1

Chair and Other Tales:
a collection

Nic Pickle

ThreeBrosProductions
2019

Supporters

I would like to thank the following people for their support of this project:

Brenda Scott Royce
Martha Perez
Roger Perez
Bradley Wigen
Jeremy Evans
PJ Repond
Elizabeth "Richie" Urbina
Rebecca Royce

Contents

Supporters iv
Prologue vii
Chair 9
Water 15
Pen 23
Chip 35
Trophy 43
Salt 51
Author 59
Epilogue 64

Prologue

Life is hard as hell, and it never gets better. There are a lot of important lessons we are never taught in life, whether it be by teachers, parents, or friends. It's these kinds of lessons that are the most important because we learn them ourselves, whether it be the easy way or the hard way. I believe all things are learned through pain, emotional or physical, doesn't matter. Pain is how we learn. The pain of mental health is the most important.

This short series of tales touches on so many subjects we never learned as children. The importance of mental health, many of the unanswered questions in life like death, or meaning. The lies we were told about love and happiness. At younger and younger ages, generations are feeling the full extent of daily struggles. Evils of the world do not always compare to the evil in your head. Thoughts of suicide flow in and out constantly. A yearning for purpose.

But in recent years media has begun to show a better portrayal of these issues. Not all people with mental health issues are serial killers, or pathetic losers who overcome the bad guy when needed. Shows like BoJack Horseman, or social media icons like Eugene, the world record egg, are constantly telling the community to seek mental help and talk to someone. But talking is the hardest part. Hopefully this strange series of inanimate objects can talk for you and teach the lessons our mentors were afraid to teach. So please, enjoy *Chair and Other Tales*.

Chair

Chair is happy

Chair is smart furniture

Chair has crush on Stool in aisle three of *Jerome's*

Chair hates Table

Table made a move on Stool

Chair killed Table's family

Chair took care of all of Table's children before Chair murdered them—each in a funnier way than the last

Chair is happy

Chair wishes to sleep

Chair cannot sleep

Chair is a piece of furniture

Chair wants to eat an avocado

Chair does not have mouth

Chair is sad

Chair does not know how Chair will kiss Stool without a mouth

Chair could grow a mouth

NEVERMIND

Chair was once tree who could grow but tree died and was left with Chair who could not

Chair just wants to sleep

Chair cannot sleep

Chair is Chair

Chair instead thinks about how Chair killed Table's family.

FIRE

Lots of fire

The memories haunt Chair

Chair wants to sleep

Chair cannot sleep

Chair is Chair

OH NO

Chair has bad news

Table is back for revenge

Table has brought reinforcements

Chair is being lifted off the ground

Chair is being taken to the back room

Chair is confused

Chair is scared

Table pushes open the door

Chair can see something in the corner

Chair can't really see what it is

Chair needs to get closer

Table's army lifts Chair higher to see the object in the corner.

OMG

Chair can now see what's in the corner

It's her, Chair's crush, **STOOL**

TABLE KILLED STOOL

Her guts are everywhere

Chair tries to turn away

Table grabs Chair's face and forces him to look

Chair begins to tear up

Chair is sad

Table laughs

And laughs

And laughs

Chair screams for help

Table laughs again

PLEASE NO

Table begins to drag Chair across the floor

Chair's leg hurts

Chair is confused

Chair is sad

Chair is angry

Chair just wants to sleep

The room is getting warmer

WHY

Chair turns to face a horrifying sight

FIRE

Table lifts Chair higher

NO TABLE, PLEASE, CHAIR WILL DO ANYTHING

Table doesn't listen

Then Table throws Chair into the fire

Chair takes one last dying breath and screams his dying words

I WILL LOVE YOU FOREVER, STOOL, AND I WILL SEE YOU IN HEAVEN

...

Then all goes dark

Is it over?

Is this what death looks like?

nothing

Just darkness for eternity

Is this death?

Chair does not know for certain

Is death different for humans than furniture?

Or is it the same?

There is no real way of knowing

Chair wishes he could *GOOGLE* it.

It doesn't matter though because Chair is dead

GOODBYE

Chair sits in silence

Chair sits in sadness

Chair misses Stool

Chair finally goes to sleep

IT IS OVER

२

Water

I awake

Rushing down the stream

I look around

Hundreds of other me's crowded in one area, each one exactly the same: H, 2, and O

But, somehow, I am different

I am alive

I mean they are alive too, but I *know* I am alive

I am... what's the word ... *sentient*

There is something inside me that allows me to know there is something inside me

But the others, they are just going with the flow and don't care

Not I

For some reason I matter

I'm important

I'm going to be a part of something bigger

The biggest thing there is

The Ocean

I need to find the ocean

"Where is the ocean?"

"That way, the end of the stream," said the fish

"But, like, where?"

"I just told you"

"I don't want to go to an ocean, I'm headed for THE ocean"

"I don't know what to tell ya, buddy. Good Luck"

The fish swims off and I am alone again.

Our stream leads into an ocean

Not THE ocean

This one is small but there is something missing

I feel unfulfilled

Luckily for me the sun comes and I leave

Everything is fluffy

Where am I?

What have I become?

I see birds

Am I a cloud?

Yes, I think I am

Being a cloud is nice, still I feel incomplete

Eventually I fall back down to another ocean

"What am I missing? I'm looking for an ocean and I've been part of two! What am I looking for?!?"

"You're probably looking for the Pacific"

I look at the crab in confusion

"What is the specific?"

"Pacific, it's an ocean. The largest one to be more specific"

"Where is it?"

"I don't know, do I look like a GPS to you?"

"What's a UPS?"

The crab rolls his eyes and walks away

Now I am a cloud again

Back to a stream

Stream to an ocean

Ocean to Cloud

And Cloud to Ocean

I am losing faith

Losing hope

I'll never find my way home

I'll be stuck in this endless cycle forever and ever

At first I was happy I was different

I thought life was a joy

A journey

But I've learned, it has no purpose

We are all just stuck in some stupid pointless cycle

Why can't it just end?

Why am I 'alive'?

What is the point of living if you never truly LIVE?

I hate myself

I don't want to be 'alive' anymore

But I don't have a choice

I am just a droplet of water

I don't want to be a part of some loser's shower

Or a glass of water left in the sun

A drip on a little girl's toothbrush that she is using to trick her dad into thinking she used it

But it doesn't matter because I will be

I have no choice

I was made sentient just as torture

I'm being tortured

…

Now, I'm on a mountain

I look around, I can see oceans in all directions

Each one I've been to

Each a dead end

But, wait

What's this?

An area I've never seen before

I roll downhill and jump into the stream

I'm on my way

In a few seconds I'll be there

The Specific Ocean

I made it

I found the ocean

It's beautiful

It's everything I expected

Fish, Plankton, Coral

This is a community

A safe haven

I dive down and find a nice shady spot

I close my eyes and sleep

…

It's hot

Very Hot

I open my eyes

OH NO

I slept too long

The current took me

It took me

It took me to the surface

I feel the sun beating on my face

NO

I try to swim down again

It is too late

I feel myself splitting apart

Changing

Evaporating

I am going to be a cloud

Again

The endless cycle is repeating again

I was almost happy

But that can never be

No one can stay happy for too long

We are stuck in a cycle

A spinning wheel

And the only way we can ever truly be happy is if someone breaks that wheel

But no one is that strong

Not a water droplet

And not a god

Is this why I was given life?

So I can hate it?

I thought I belonged

I was wrong

I give up

I close my eyes

Pen

'What am I supposed to do with this?'

He said, holding me in his hand

'Write with it'

'Yeah, I got that. When you said you had a gift for me I thought it would be a little something more than just a pen'

'It's not just a pen, it's a fountain pen'

I'm special?

I thought

YAY

I like feeling special

'What does that mean?'

'It's a cool kind of pen that they used to use in the olden days'

'Cool'

I watch him roll his eyes

'Just imagine, everything used to be done with this kind of pen'

'I don't care'

'No computers, or texting'

'Dad, you're talking like some old dude'

'People used to write books with these, ENTIRE BOOKS!'

What's a book?

Can I write one, too?

I'm going to write a book

'Fine, I'll take the pen'

'Good, and what do you say?'

'Thank you'

'You're welcome'

'Dad' left the room

It's just me and him now

So, what are we going to do?

Can we write a book?

It's always been my dream to write a book

Can we?

I wait for an answer

He didn't hear me

But he does look at me

Turns me around

Rubs my side with his thumb

Suddenly I am in the air

Wind rushing past me

I am flying down

Then I stop

I land on some fuzz

Everything seems taller now

Next to me is a big dark cavern

The place looks scary

It is filled with old toys and dirty socks

I wonder what this place is called

I do not wish to go in there

It is not my dream

I look up at him

He is sitting on a spinning seat

I don't know what to call it

I don't know much yet

The names of things elude me

WHOA

What is an 'elude' and how did I know it?

I think I'm getting smarter

Maybe one day I will be smart enough to follow my dream

...

It's boring here

On the fuzz

All he does is sit in his swivel thing

And stare at his screen

It's boring sitting and waiting for something to happen

It's boring waiting for your dream to come

I don't want to wait

I want to *do*

But he doesn't

I can't write a book without him

I can't move

I can't do anything

It's hard to achieve a dream when you are stuck where you are

OH!

Achieve!!

I learned another one

One day I will use 'Achieve' and 'Elude' in my book

It will be perfect

...

He still hasn't done anything

I've been here a long time

All he does is walk past me from the fuzz floor to the flat mountain on top of the cavern

He seems to like it up there

Is it soft there?

He looks at his screen there, too

'Hello?'

Is he talking to me?

'Hey, Whattup?'

No, he isn't

I got my hopes up

I'm let down now

'Oh, nothing. I'm just chilling on my bed'

GASP

Is that what it's called?

Bed?

He likes to sleep on top of Mountain Bed

I shall mention Mountain Bed in my book

But I won't mention its dark cavern

It's scary

'Yeah, sure. I'll be on my way'

I hear him moving up there

I roll my eyes like he does

He is just going to pass by me again

Like he always does

But then he doesn't

Instead of his foot going right next to me

It lands on top of me

'OW!'

He steps off suddenly

'That freakin hurt!'

He kicks me

'Thank god I wasn't wearing shoes, Dad would have killed me if stain this carpet'

I never take my eyes off him, because I already know what's happening

I don't want to look around

It's dark here

He opens his door and leaves

I'm alone

I'm alone under the bed

I don't want to look around

I want to stop looking and dream

He walks in

But not him

The big him, the one who I used to be with

Big Him is looking for something

'Son?'

I wonder what it is

'Son, where are you?'

I wonder if Big Him had dreams

Did he ever give up?

I want to give up

Under Mountain Bed is scary

My dream is not here

Where is his dream?

'SON!!!'

Is 'Son' his dream?

Is he looking for his dream, too?

Big Him begins to grumble and storms out of the room

I listen and hear Big Him drive away

I wonder where he is going

I think I shall rest

...

'DAD!'

I wake up

'DAD! Where you at! I'm hungry!!'

He is back and looking for something

Maybe he is looking for me

'DAD!!!'

I'm here!!!

He doesn't hear me again

But there is something we both hear

BOOM!!!

'Dad?'

What was that?

'DAD!?!'’

He runs outside again

That was a loud noise; I wonder what happened

I hear him crying outside

I feel like crying

...

Boxes are everywhere

He is packing things up

The room is empty now

He is crying again

Did he lose his dream?

I think I've lost mine, too

Dreams don't come true

I've waited so long

And for nothing

I will never write a book

I will always be stuck under Mountain Bed

Then he grabs me

My heart jumps

He pulls me into the light

'What the…?'

He looks at me

He begins to cry again

Why did looking at me make him cry?

'It's all my fault'

What is?

'It's all my fault'

He can't hear me

'He went out looking for me'

'He was driving at the same time that drunk idiot was'

I don't know what he is talking about

'It's all my fault'

He wipes his tears on his shirt sleeve and looks at me

He stands up suddenly

I'm in the air again

We go to his now empty desk

He rips out a piece of paper from his notebook

My cap is bitten off and he spits it to the other side of the room

This is it

The moment I have been waiting for

We are going to write a book

We begin

'Dedicated to Da--'

Something bad happens

I feel sick

He begins to shake me

Bang me against the desk

I feel empty inside

I'm so close to my dream, but something inside of me just...

Doesn't want it

Dreams don't come true

I know that now

Something better than that is down the road

So long as you don't give up

'I give up'

What!?

He tosses me to the floor and stands

NO, you can't do this to me

He continues packing

NO NO NO NO

He can't hear me

The room is almost completely empty now

He forgot I'm here

But he walks in one last time

He doesn't see it, but I do

I see his foot, coming down on me just like last time

CRACK!

At least I can't stain the carpet anymore

Chip

There we were

Happy together

We had seen others leave before, and we knew one day that would be us

I didn't realize it would be so soon

It had gotten colder recently

More and more of us were being put into the room more and more often

I've played that day over and over again

We had no idea what was in that room

We thought it was something good

It wasn't

We were grabbed, the whole lot of us

The doors opened

I caught a glimpse inside

It was a small room with a plate of coals in the middle of it

The roof seemed to reach upwards forever

We were dropped onto the plate

And I broke off from the group

We were dropped so hard that I flew

I landed on a little ridge in the brick wall above the plate

I was about to jump down and join the rest of the log colony, when the coals exploded

Fire came from below

Before we were happy together

Now they were dying together

I was the luckiest chip in the bunch

They burned in front of me

And I couldn't help them

I just froze

And watched

I didn't try to help

And then they were gone

I could have helped

But I didn't

I didn't do anything

Did I even care?

They were my family

My colony

My log

We were happy together

Now I'm sad and alone

I replay that day over and over in my head

And every day

Every single day

Another log is put into the room with me

The looks of excitement on their wooden faces

Then the surprise when everything gets warm

Then the look of horror when they die

They go from a large colony to a small pile of ash

And I don't warn them

I just watch them

No emotions

I couldn't save my family

Why should I save someone else's?

But every time I watch it, I'm sad when it's over

I could have done something

But I didn't want to

I don't want them to be alive

Maybe I don't want to be alive

Is my life worth living if it's just spent watching others end?

Is life worth living if it's just spent waiting for something that never comes?

Is life worth living if you are with people?

If you aren't happy together?

Is life worth living if there isn't anything after?

I don't think I want to be alive

I don't see the point

Yeah, sure, I'm safe from death

But what's the point

What's the point of living if it's just spent not dying?

Sure, you may be happy

But once you die, does that happiness matter?

Survivor's remorse, I guess

I blame myself

They died and I didn't

I should've

And now I want to

But every time another log is put into the flame

I don't have the guts to jump from my ledge

Hanging up here thinking

All day every day

Thinking

Thinking about being happy together

I think that everyone wants to die

But nobody wants to be dead

I want to die

I want to be with the rest of them

Unless there isn't anything

Unless they are gone forever

But what else do I have to do?

Either sit here until I rot watching other wood chips like me die

Or die with them and no longer exist

What if there's nothing?

What if there's everything?

What if it doesn't matter?

If I die I will either be in heaven and suffer with the things that I've seen forever

Or there is nothing

What if there is a third option?

A limbo

Do I even care?

I just don't want to be here anymore

But I don't want the risk of nothing

I want to die

But I don't want to be dead

I want to jump

But I don't want to burn

I want to be happy

But I don't know if I can again

...

It has been many days and many nights here

I've tried to jump

I've tried to do it

But today is the day

The door opens and another log is placed inside

I look at their happy faces

Oh, are they in for a treat

Then I hear their screams

Then the screams stop

I didn't do it

WHY CAN'T I JUMP!?!

Tomorrow

...

Three tomorrows later and nothing

I haven't done it

I haven't grasped the concept of not living yet

And another log is placed in the room

Happy

Screams

Silence

Tomorrow

Happy

Screams

Silence

Tomorrow

Happy

Screams

Silence

Tomorrow

Happy

Screams

Jump

Rushing wind

Screams

Intense Heat

I open my eyes

I look around

And I'm happy

I'm happy that we are now dying together

Happy Together and then darkness

…

Trophy

Trophy is new

Trophy is shiny

Trophy is useless

Trophy sat on a table for 5 hours

Trophy had no clue what was happening

Trophy didn't know anything yet

The curtain in front of Trophy slowly rolls open

Trophy looks to the other Trophies around him

They all seem smaller than him

Trophy realizes he is different

Trophy is thinking

More than them

They don't think

They just sit

Trophy looks forward again

In front of him is a crowd of people

A human walks on stage with him and begins to make noises

Trophy doesn't understand the noises

One by one the woman hands the other trophies to the humans in the crowd until Trophy is the last one

Then he comes on stage

He looks extremely awkward

'Aren't you happy?'

WHOA!

Trophy understood that

Trophy wonders what 'happy' is

The awkward boy shakes his head up and down

The woman grabs trophy and lifts him up

Awkward boy takes Trophy into his hands

The boy walks with Trophy off the stage and they sit in a chair together

The woman makes more noises and the curtain closes

As the night comes to an end Trophy and the boy get into the back of the car and go home

The boy maintains the same face the entire time

Trophy wants to know what happy is

Is boy happy?

Trophy doesn't know yet

Yet

Boy and Trophy get to Boy's room

Boy sits on his bed and looks at Trophy

Boy smiles

Trophy smiles back but boy does not see

Boy places Trophy on a shelf overlooking the rest of the room

Boy goes to bed and leaves Trophy in the dark

Boy seems Happy

Trophy still doesn't understand Happy, but Trophy feels good about making Boy smile

The room is dark

Trophy glistens every time a car drives past the window.

Trophy feels special

...

As time goes on, Trophy gets dusty as he watches Boy grow up

Trophy understands more and more things every day

Trophy still does not understand Happy

Trophy understands Joy, Cheer, Glee

But a state of Happy eludes Trophy

Trophy has seen Gloom, Depression

But not sadness

...

Boy is no longer a Boy

Boy is now Half-Boy, Half-Man

Halfie

Trophy no longer brings Halfie joy

Girl Halfie once brought Boy Halfie joy

But Girl Halfie left

Boy Halfie was depressed

Trophy would watch Boy do work, after being gone all day

One day Halfie turned into Young Man

And Young Man stopped doing work

Young Man came home and did nothing

Young Man said he would do something

He did not

Young Man had dreams he said would make him happy

Young Man said he didn't need school

Trophy watched Young Man get more depressed

But there were some Joyous moments

Never in a state of Happy

Or Sad

Trophy watched Young Man be gloomy over his dead parents, and gleeful about his new house that he got from them

Trophy got less and less shiny and new

And so did Boy

He went through pill troubles, money troubles, relationship troubles

Trophy feels bad

Trophy misses the Boy, and Trophy is sure Young Man does too

...

Young Man had grown into Man

Trophy is more dusty

Man had found Woman

They spend a lot of time together

They make each other feel joy

But still neither are happy

Even when they have a Boy of their own

And a girl, too

Trophy has spent all these years trying to understand Happy

Trophy has heard it so many times, it means nothing now

One small moment of Joy is somehow Happy in people's eyes

But it isn't

Happy is a state

Sad is a state

Joy, Glee, Cheer are emotions

Gloom is an emotion

Happy is not real

Happy is an idea created to make people feel better, but it does the opposite

Everyone wants to be happy

They are depressed when they can't be happy

You cannot be something that does not exist

Trophy does not bring Happy

Trophy brings Joy

Trophy brings Glee and Cheer

Not having Trophy brings Gloom

Not having Trophy brings Depression

Trophy does not make someone Happy

Happy is made

Sad is made

Made up

Trophy now understands

Man, Woman, Boy, and Girl bring each other joy, sometimes gloom

They do not need Trophy to make Happy

Trophy is eventually thrown into the trash

Trophy is melted

Trophy leaves

Trophy stops existing, and does so unhappily

Salt

I'm constantly shaken until there's nothing inside

I'm a simple salt shaker

But I'm somehow alive

I don't know how, but I am

I am aware of my surroundings

But feel nothing

On the outside, I'm white with a cartoon smile painted on my side

I look happy

On the inside I'm nothing

On the outside I'm okay

On the inside I'm just salt, the bare necessity for my existence, but anything else?

No

Nothing inside

But I play it off as if there is

I act like I feel emotions but I don't

I don't care

I pretend to worry about others

I pretend to be sad when others are

I pretend to happy when I'm not

There is a whole spice rack of others with emotions

Chili powder has a spicy personality

Cinnamon is a nuisance

But cinnamon sugar is someone you always want around

Nutmeg is just a yes man

Garlic is tough, but will help you out when you need it

Saffron is just a bitch

They all seem to be exactly like the little faces painted on their sides

It's hard living like this

These labels and masks hide who we really are

If they could all see that I'm not happy

But I put on the same smile, and no one knows how I feel

'Hi there, cutie!'

I turn around and see her

'My name's Pepper'

'Salt'

'I'm new here, but you seem nice; mind showing me around?'

'Course!'

I begin to show her around the kitchen

She looks just like me

Same painted smile

We were made for each other

...

Days follow as Pepper and I grow closer

Her beautiful smile

I always feel bad, I want to show her how I truly feel inside, but I can't

I've never shared anything about myself with anyone

Why should I share with her?

What if we get separated?

I'll spend the rest of my life knowing the only person I opened up to, just left

That would hurt

So, I won't do it

I'll just keep smiling like her

...

Life goes on and we're still together

Closer than ever

Then she says it

'I Love You'

I don't know what to say

I've never said those words before and meant it

I can say them no problem

After all they are just words

I don't think those words mean anything

They're just a lie

But the pressure is building

An awkward moment passes

And so I lie

'I Love You Too'

Why did I say that!?

I know I didn't mean it

I can't

I don't feel anything

But I just said it

And now I'm stuck

I dug myself into a hole

I can't take it back

I'm a liar and a fake

Emotions on the outside, nothing on the inside

A painted smile

Another lie

I'm lying to her and myself

...

Humans get married all the time

But I'm a salt shaker

I can't feel love

So, what's the point?

Pepper wants to get married

So, I act like I want to too

I don't want to be with her anymore

It's constantly eating at me that I lied

Maybe if I told the truth, I might love her today

But I don't

Not today, not ever

I don't even love myself

This is all that ever runs through my head

A constant rant

It's all my fault

All I do is lie to myself and everyone

I'm fake

Emotions are hard alright

I can't deal with this

I'm not like everyone else

I can't process my emotions as easily

Love is a lie

And all I do is lie

I'm stuck

Stuck in an emotionless relationship with a pepper shaker

My mind boggles as to why I can't say the words I want to say

Are the words wrong?!

Or am I afraid what everyone else will think?

All I wanted in life was someone to share how I felt with, but all I can do is fake smile

Nothing on the inside

Everyone thinks I'm happy

But I'm not

The happiest people are actually the saddest

But no one can tell

And no one will tell

Pepper and I will grow old together and just lie to each other till we get thrown into the trash

I'm not brave enough to break up with her because I'm not brave enough to say why.

And then I'll die

With this fake smile on my face.

Author

He sits alone in his crumby little apartment

Wearing the same clothes he slept in

And wore the day before

And slept in the night before

He doesn't change his clothes, because why should he?

He never goes out

He just sits at his desk in his apartment

He says he forgets to shave but really he just doesn't feel like it

On his desk is a computer that never turns off

A box of tissues he should use instead of his shirt

A ton of empty bottles with their bottoms sticky because that little bit of beverage he didn't drink just kinda disappeared leaving behind sugar and syrup

His dirty plates in front of the TV currently paused on his ninth run of *Parks and Recreation*

He spends his days writing stories

Stories of depressed characters

Stories with serious messages that don't always seem to get across

He never talks to his parents because why should he

His dad doesn't approve of anything he does and his mom has her career to worry about, not his

His siblings are more successful than him

A Doctor

A Composer

And then there's him.

The rundown author

Failed script-writer

Yeah, he had a show

It was the story of a man who had the perfect life, but couldn't get over his past

Mental Health Issues, and messed-up past

He spends all his time worried about then, and ends up ruining the now

He doesn't realize he ruined everything, until it's too late

It was a great show

Everyone hailed his storytelling abilities, but no one realized the truth

The story was about him

He was praised for being creative

It isn't creativity if it's the truth

But no one realized that

So, he wrote 'Chair'

A short story about a Chair wondering what death is like

Chair was a hit

So, he made Water

Then Pen, Chip, Trophy, Salt, and so on

All of them big hits

Talking about real issues, through objects

It worked for a little while

It was his way of telling the world how he felt again

But just like last time, no one understood the truth

No one had any idea he was tired of living in a cycle

...

He spends all his days working and texting old friends who never respond

And when they do respond, it's to invite him out

But he doesn't want to go out

Dating is hard because humans need to communicate

He can't communicate

Not unless it's through his characters

But then people wouldn't understand

He's conflicted at all times

He spends his nights thinking about how he should be spending his days, but by the time morning rolls around he does nothing

So many people say that if you struggle with mental health, just talk

Some of them don't understand how hard it is

It's even harder when you have no one to talk to

Especially when it comes to suicide

If you were to tell a police officer you want to kill yourself, they will arrest you and take you to a mental health facility

If he can't trust the police who can he trust?

He tells himself he has no one

When there are so many people who want to be with him

But he pushes them away because he thinks he doesn't deserve it.

His rent is due soon

He needs cash

His agent tells him people are kinda getting sick of the inanimate object thing

He should write something original

But what?

He's never done that before

Everything he has written was about himself

He sits thinking

He looks at his lamp in the corner

'Hi, what are you thinking?'

And then he begins to write

Epilogue

And so, the book comes to an end, with Chair dead, Water never seeing the Pacific, Pen losing its dream, Chip burning, Trophy being recycled, Salt stuck in a loveless relationship, and the Author stuck in his sad life and depressed mental state.

I hope you enjoyed this collection of stories and share them with others and share how you feel about them as well. The point of these stories is not to make money, but to vent. Exposing the truths of this world, and hopefully not being too preachy about it. And remember Chair is dead, so stop asking for a sequel. This book is all you get!!

Sincerely,

Nic Pickle

CPSIA information can be obtained
at www.ICGtesting.com
Printed in the USA
BVHW031625010619
549794BV00017B/21/P